I USED TO BE FAMOUS

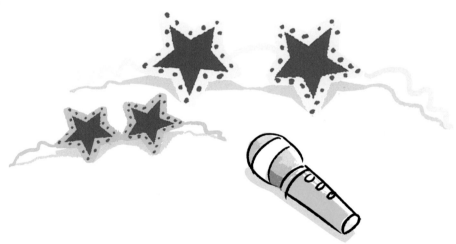

by **Tara Luebbe** and **Becky Cattie**

pictures by **Joanne Lew-Vriethoff**

Albert Whitman & Company
Chicago, Illinois

To our mom, the photographer, and dad, the videographer.
Thanks for always making us feel famous.—TL & BC

To my 3 M's, you will always be famous to me—JLV

Library of Congress Cataloging-in-Publication data is on file with the publisher.

Text copyright © 2019 by Tara Luebbe and Becky Cattie
Pictures copyright © 2019 by Joanne Lew-Vriethoff
First published in the United States of America in 2019 by Albert Whitman & Company
ISBN 978-0-8075-3443-4

Printed in China
10 9 8 7 6 5 4 3 2 1 WKT 24 23 22 21 20 19

For more information about Albert Whitman & Company,
visit our website at www.albertwhitman.com.

100 Years of Albert Whitman & Company
Celebrate with us in 2019!

I am famous.

I'm a triple threat. In showbiz, that means
I'm multitalented.

I have a personal shopper,

a sensational biography,

and a star on the Sidewalk of Fame.

And because I am famous, the paparazzi are always taking pictures of me.

Showtime!

Hey! Where *are* the paparazzi?
My fans?

Is it that new celebrity in town?
Could she be more famous than me?

Aunt Mimi? Grandma? Grandpa? Hey, that's MY fan club!

I have no choice. I must confront this moppet.

You can't act

or dance.

You call that singing?

You have no fashion sense.

What's that smell?
Eau de poo poo?

Look kid, I'm the star of this show.
Always have been.
Always will be.
I will not be upstaged by an amateur.

Do I need a new act?

What about a new look?

A new audience?

I *used* to be famous.

You win, kid. You've outshined me.

I'm washed up. In showbiz, that means I used to be a big deal but not anymore. You're the star now. Good luck.

Why are you laughing at me? It's not funny.
I'll show you funny.

Oh! I have a new fan.
Watch this! And this!

Okay, I guess you are a teeny-tiny bit cute.

Maybe I should help this little starlet.
It's important for famous people to be good
role models.

I'll start with her hair and clothes, and give her dance lessons.

I'll teach her to sing.

I'll give her a part in my new musical. I've always wanted to be a director. They call all the shots.

Hmm...a co-star?

Look! It's the paparazzi!
They LOVE us.

Maybe sharing the spotlight
isn't so bad.

Above all, the show *must* go on!

Wake up, baby, it's showtime!

We are famous.